Published and distributed by

ISLAND HERITAGE™
P U B L I S H I N G

94-411 KOʻAKI STREET, WAIPAHU, HAWAIʻI 96797-2806
ORDERS: (800) 468-2800 • INFORMATION: (808) 564-8800
FAX: (808) 564-8877 • www.islandheritage.com

ISBN# : 0-89610-350-1

First Edition, Fourth Printing - 2008

LITTLE PRINCESS KA'IULANI
IN HER GARDEN BY THE SEA

By Ellie Crowe

Illustrated by Mary Koski

DEDICATION

For Micah and Luke with love.

As from your house your mother sees
You playing round the garden trees,
So you may see, if you will look
Through the windows of this book,
Another child, far, far away,
And in another garden, play.

"A Child's Garden of Verses"
— Robert Louis Stevenson

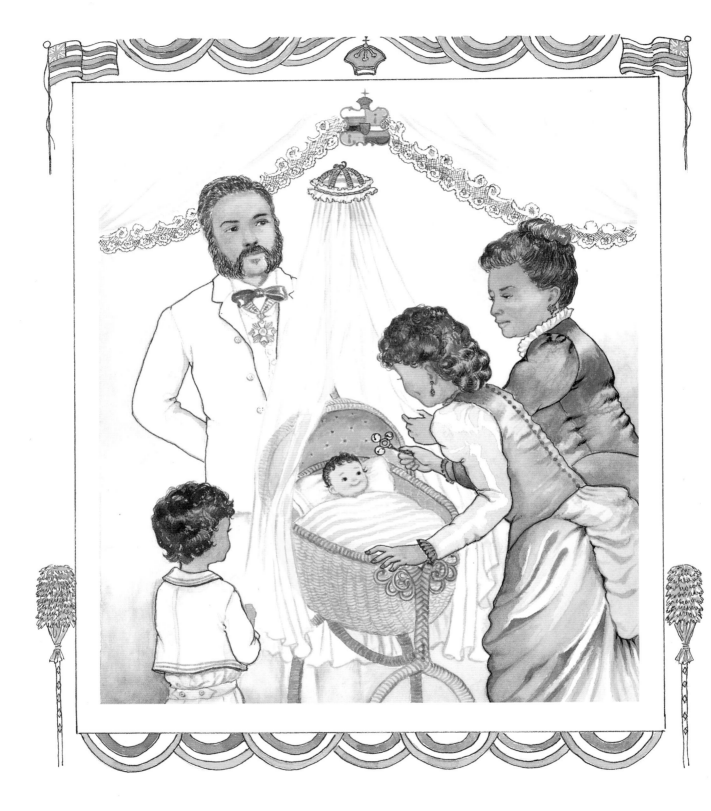

Long, long ago a mighty family of chiefs and chieftesses ruled the islands of Hawai'i. They were called the Ali'i. The Ali'i were very unhappy. There were no royal babies. There was no one to grow up and sit on the throne of the great King Kamehameha.

Then a wonderful thing happened — I was born! A baby princess! Everyone was very excited. Bells pealed all day and cannons boomed. I don't know how I managed to sleep through it!

I was christened on Christmas Day. They gave me a very long name, Victoria Kawekiu Lunalilo Kalaninuiahilapalapa Ka'iulani. It took me years to learn how to spell it!

The name Ka'iulani means "the royal sacred one" so that was rather nice.

My happy aunt, the Princess Ruth, gave me a beautiful garden by the sea. My mother, Princess Likelike, carried me there when I was very small.

"There's a lovely cool breeze blowing here from the valley of Mānoa," she said. "Let's call this place 'Āinahau, which means Land of Cool Breezes." So they did.

My father looked at the beautiful green fields.

"Let's plant a banyan tree," he said. "Then Ka'iulani can play and sit in its shade." So they did.

I loved to play in my garden by the sea. I fed the fishes in the lily pond. I liked to chase the fat brown frogs.

"Better hop faster, Bufo," I said, "or my giant turtle will catch you." My turtle had such a snapping mouth, I had to be careful when I fed him.

One morning when I woke up I heard strange wailing cries. "Auwē!" I said. "That sounds like nightmarchers." I hid my head under the blankets.

"Get up, Ka'iulani," called my mother. "Come and see your pet peacock."

The peacock had shimmering blue and green plumes. "He's so beautiful," I said. I fetched some crumbs and the peacock fed right out of my hand. "Let's get lots and lots of peacocks." So they did.

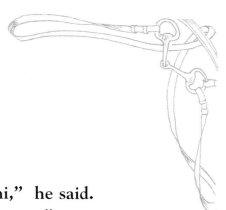

One day my father called me. "Ka'iulani," he said.
"Close your eyes. I have a special surprise for you."

I shut my eyes very tight. I heard strange clomping noises
so I sneaked a peep out of the corner of one eye . . . and there
was a snow white pony.

"Oh! Oh!" I cried. "I love him!" I patted his warm nose
and looked into his deep brown eyes. "I'm going to call him
Fairy."

Sometimes we would sit under the banyan tree and have concerts. I would play my ʻukulele. My aunt, Princess Liliʻuokalani, and my uncles, Prince Kalākaua and Prince Leleiohoku, loved to sing. The birds in the mango trees would all sing too.

On a very important day my uncle, Prince Kalākaua, became King. I climbed on a chair and peered out of the palace window at the crowds cheering below. My mother came running into the room.

"Quick!" she cried. "Come and march in the procession." That was fun! The band played *Hawaiʻi Ponoʻī* and everyone wore their very best clothes.

The new King wore a white helmet with red, white and blue plumes and a white uniform. He looked very grand.

This is Saint Andrew's where I went to church and prayed to be good. I'm sorry to tell you that sometimes I was very naughty.

Once I said to my governess, "No! I won't listen to you. I won't do what you say."

"You have to listen to me," my governess replied.

"No!" I cried. "My mother says that princesses don't have to listen to governesses."

"Even princesses have to obey the rules, Ka'iulani," said my governess. So I did.

My friend Elsie and I made leis out of Pikake flowers. I liked to wear these because they smelled so sweet. I was called "The Princess of the Peacocks" because pikake means *peacock* in the Hawaiian language. I liked that.

Once when we were playing, Elsie waved the pikake branch. It cut me just above my eye. Blood dripped onto my white dress.

"What happened?" my mother asked. She was very angry and Elsie was afraid.

"Nothing happened. It was an accident, Mama," I said.

"I'm sorry, Ka'iulani," Elsie said later. "I won't play with sticks again."

Sometimes my friends and I made sand castles in the sand. We tried to build a castle like 'Iolani Palace.

I had a friend who was a poet. He wrote beautiful poems and told wonderful stories. His name was Robert Louis Stevenson but sometimes he was called "Tusitala" or "Teller of Tales." He wrote a very exciting story called *Treasure Island.*

We sat in a grass shack under the palm trees and he told me about his country, Scotland, and about England where I would be sent to school one day.

He wrote this poem for me:

Forth from her land to mine she goes,
The island maid, the island rose,
Light of heart and bright of face,
The daughter of a double race.

Her islands here in southern sun
Shall mourn their Ka'iulani gone,
And I, in her dear banyan's shade,
Look vainly for my little maid.

But our Scots islands far away
Shall glitter with unwonted day.
And cast for once their tempests by
To smile in Ka'iulani's eye.

—Robert Louis Stevenson

I liked his poem but I didn't want to go to school in his cold country far away from my garden.

Sometimes dark clouds gathered over the pali. I liked the storm. I stood on the shore and looked out at the rain falling on the sea.

England was somewhere far over those waters. I would go there when I was 14 years old. I would be brave and strong. I would make many new friends and tell them about my wonderful island kingdom. I would always try to do what was right.

Sometimes being a princess is wonderful and sometimes it is very hard, but I'll always remember I was so happy in my garden by the sea.

BIBLIOGRAPHY

Daws, Gavan. *A History of the Hawaiian Islands*. Honolulu. University of Hawaii Press, 1968.

Marantz, Maxine. *R. L. Stevenson: Poet in Paradise*. Honolulu. Aloha Graphic and Sales, 1977.

McGaw, Martha Mary. *Stevenson in Hawaii*. Honolulu, University of Hawaii Press, 1950.

Webb, Nancy and Jean Francis. *Ka'iulani: Crown Princess of Hawaii*. The Viking Press Inc., 1962.

Zambucka, Kristen. *Princess Ka'iulani: The Last Hope of Hawaii's Monarchy*. Honolulu. Mana Publishing Company, 1982.